Scared
Silly

Scared Silly

by **James Howe**

illustrated by **Jeff Mack**

Atheneum Books for Young Readers
New York London Toronto Sydney

Harold is a special dog in many ways. He reads, he writes, and he loves chocolate. But chocolate is not a good food for most dogs; in fact, it makes them sick. Share your chocolate with people only. And give your dog another kind of treat—one that's just right for him or her.

Atheneum Books for Young Readers
An imprint of Simon & Schuster Children's Publishing Division
1230 Avenue of the Americas, New York, New York 10020
This book is a work of fiction. Names, characters, places, and incidents are either products of the author's imagination or are used fictitiously. Any resemblance to actual events or locales or persons, living or dead, is entirely coincidental.
Text copyright © 1989, 2005 by James Howe
Illustrations copyright © 2005 by Jeff Mack
Text adapted by Heather Henson from *Scared Silly: A Halloween Treat* by James Howe
All rights reserved, including the right of reproduction in whole or in part in any form.
READY-TO-READ is a registered trademark of Simon & Schuster, Inc.
Book design by Abelardo Martínez
The text for this book is set in Century Old Style.
The illustrations for this book are rendered in acrylic.
Manufactured in the United States of America
First Edition
10 9 8 7 6 5 4 3 2 1
Library of Congress Cataloging-in-Publication Data
Howe, James, 1946-
Scared silly / James Howe ; illustrated by Jeff Mack.— 1st ed.
p. cm. — (Bunnicula and friends ; #3)
Summary: Harold, Chester, and Howie have a harrowing Halloween night worrying about Bunnicula as well as about a witch who comes into the house.
ISBN 0-689-85726-8
[1. Halloween—Fiction. 2. Dogs—Fiction. 3. Cats—Fiction. 4. Rabbits—Fiction.] I. Mack, Jeff, ill. II. Title. III. Series.
PZ7.H83727Sc 2005
[Fic]—dc22
2004010538

With love to my daughter, Zoey,
born in the Year of the Rabbit
—J. H.

For my gram
—J. M.

CHAPTER 1

Spooky Halloween

Halloween is always spooky at our house.

There are grinning pumpkins and scary costumes and tricky tricks and yummy treats.

Of course the treats are my favorite part.

Especially the chocolate ones.

I live with the Monroes—Toby,
Pete, and Mr. and Mrs. Monroe.
They are human, but I don't hold that
against them.

Chester lives here too. He's a cat. Enough said.

Howie is a puppy, and Bunnicula is a rabbit.

Rabbits don't usually do much.

Hop around. Wiggle their whiskers. Look cute.

The thing is, Bunnicula is no ordinary rabbit, but more about him later.

As I was saying, Halloween can be spooky around here.

But this year things were even spookier than usual.

It all started when the Monroes left us alone.

"Where have they gone this time?" Howie whimpered.

He hates to be left alone.

"I think they said something about a costume party," I said with a yawn.

"I guess they have better things to do than sleep," Chester said.

I yawned again. "What could be better than sleep? Except eating, of course."

"Harold, you should really try to stay awake," Chester said.

"Why?" I asked.

"Because it's a dark and stormy night!" Chester cried.

"So?"

"So, don't you remember what happened on that other dark and stormy night?" Chester demanded.

I thought about it for a minute.

"Lightning?"

Chester nodded.

"Thunder?"

Chester nodded again.

"In that case, I was definitely under the covers—asleep!"

"No, you weren't," Chester said. "You were standing right beside me when they brought that monster home."

"M-m-m-monster?" Howie asked.

"He means Bunnicula." I sighed.

Chester blames Bunnicula for all the strange things that go on around here. And believe me, a lot of strange things go on around here.

"That rabbit is up to something, I just know it," Chester said.

We all turned to look at Bunnicula.

He was sitting in his cage, wide awake.

Bunnicula is awake only at night.

Chester says it's because he's a vampire bunny.

I don't argue with Chester. It's bad for my health.

"I have a plan," Chester said.

"No! No plans!" I cried.

Chester's plans are *really* bad for my health.

"This plan is simple. Nothing to it," Chester said. "All you have to do is sit here and keep an eye on Bunnicula."

"Why?" I groaned.

"Because it's Halloween!" Chester cried. "Who knows what vampire bunnies get up to on Halloween?"

CHAPTER 2

Trick or Treat

I have to admit keeping an eye on Bunnicula sounded simple enough.
So I settled down on the sofa.
I watched Bunnicula.
He watched me.
In no time I was fast asleep.

When I woke up it had gotten
darker—and noisier.

The wind was howling.

The walls were creaking.

Something was rattling.

"That noise sounds like skeleton
bones," Chester said.

"I think they're Howie's teeth,"
I said.

"W-w-w-what's going on out there?"
Howie asked. He was looking out the
window. "W-w-w-who are *they*?"

"Oh, nobody," Chester said. "Just some goblins looking for puppies to have as a midnight snack."

Howie yelped and dived behind the couch.

"You're scaring Howie," I said to Chester.

Chester shrugged. "What's Halloween without being scared silly?"

"Come on out, Howie," I said. "There really aren't any goblins. It's just kids out trick-or-treating."

"They didn't look like kids to me," Howie said.

"That's the point," I told him. "They're wearing costumes."

"Why?"

"That's what kids do on Halloween," I explained.

"Chester was just trying to scare you," I continued. "But there's really nothing to be scared about."

At that very moment, the lights went out.

"Except maybe the dark," I said and joined Howie behind the couch.

"W-w-w-who turned out the lights?" Howie whimpered.

"I don't know," Chester said. "But I'll bet that rabbit had something to do with it."

Howie and I peeked at Bunnicula.

He was sitting up in his cage, staring at us.

I must admit he looked kind of strange.

His eyes gleamed red.

His little fangs glistened.

"W-w-w-what kind of rabbits have fangs?" Howie asked.

"The vampire kind!" Chester hissed.

We all kept staring at Bunnicula, and he stared right back.

In no time I was sleepy again. I let out a big yawn. So did Howie.

"Stop looking into his eyes!" Chester cried. "That must be part of his terrible plan! He's trying to make us fall asleep!"

"Not a bad plan," I said.

I was just about to slip into another cozy nap, when all of a sudden there was a loud *tap. Tap. Tap.*

"W-w-what's that?" Howie gulped.

"Somebody's knocking at the door!" Chester whispered.

Tap. Tap. Tap.

"Maybe it's a friend of Bunnicula's!" Chester cried.

"Maybe it's a tree branch," I said.

Tap. Tap. Tap.

"There are no trees near the front door," Chester replied.

Chester was right. I hate it when Chester is right.

Tap. Tap. Tap.

"Maybe it's a trick-or-treater," I said.

Slowly, the doorknob began to turn.

"I don't think so," Chester answered.

"W-w-w-who's at the door?" Howie whispered.

"It's just the wind," I said.

The door flew open.

"Uncle Harold?" Howie whispered.

"Yes?"

"D-d-d-does the wind wear a pointy hat?"

"No, but witches do," Chester said.

CHAPTER 3

Witch's Brew

Chester was right—again.

It *was* a witch, and she was standing right in the middle of our living room!

She wore a long black cape and a pointy black hat.

She had a crooked nose and hairy warts.

She rubbed her hands together and—

Bang!

—the front door slammed shut.

"Help!" Howie yelped.

"What was that?" the witch croaked in a creaky voice.

She whirled around. Her eyes darted about the room.

"Is anybody here?" she asked.

Nobody said a word. Nobody breathed.

The witch shrugged.

"What a night! What a night!"
she said, cackling.

Then she picked up a jack-o'-lantern,
lit the candle inside, and took it with her
into the kitchen.

"What is she doing here?" Howie whined. "Why would she pick our house?"

"There's only one reason I can think of," Chester said, glancing toward the rabbit cage.

"Bunnicula?" Howie asked.

Chester nodded. "The vampire rabbit and the witch. They're in cahoots."

"I thought we lived in Centerville," said Howie.

"Cahoots isn't a place," sighed Chester. "It means they're cooking something up together."

Just then we heard the bang of pots and pans in the kitchen.

"Maybe it's fudge," I said.

"Don't get your hopes up," replied Chester.

As quietly as we could we crept across the floor and nudged the kitchen door open.

The room was glowing with candles.

Something was bubbling in a pot on the stove.

"What is it?" Howie whispered.

"Witch's brew," said Chester.

The witch began to stir the pot. She was singing a strange tune in a creaky, crackly voice.

"Spells," Chester said. "Chants! Bubble, bubble, toil, and trouble!"

Suddenly the witch stopped singing. She stopped stirring. She lifted her nose and sniffed.

"Now where are those animals?" she croaked.

We were out of there!

We ran back to the living room faster than you can say "trick-or-treat!"

"W-w-w-what are we going to do?" Howie whimpered.

Chapter 4

Harold to the Rescue

"Chester, this is one time I hope you have a plan," I said.

"The plan is to get out of here," Chester replied.

"Sounds good to me," I said.

Just then the kitchen door swung open.

The witch walked back into the room. She was clicking her tongue as she looked this way and that.

"What is she doing?" Howie asked.

"I think she's trying to put a spell on us," said Chester.

The witch was coming closer and closer! Then she stopped.

"Ah, Bunnicula!" she said, cackling.

Carefully she lifted the rabbit out of his cage and carried him into the kitchen.

"See?" Chester cried. "Bunnicula and the witch are in this together."

"I don't think so," I said. Suddenly I was worried—not about us, but about Bunnicula.

"What do you mean?" Chester cried.

"I don't know," I answered. "It's just the way the little guy looked at me when the witch picked him up."

"He was trying to put you into a trance again!" Chester said. "It's what vampires do!"

I crept out from behind the sofa and headed back to the kitchen.

"What are you doing?" Chester cried.

"We've got to save Bunnicula," I said.

"We've got to save *us!*" said Chester. "I'm getting out of here as fast as I can."

"How?" I wanted to know.

"Through the pet door," Chester said.

"And where is the pet door?" I asked.

"In the kitchen," Chester answered. "But I'm not lifting a paw to help that creature."

"I'll help, Uncle Harold," Howie said.

"Good pup. All you need to do is distract the witch. I'll get the bunny."

Once more we crept to the kitchen
door.

Then we made a run for it.

"Oh, my stars!" cried the witch.

She threw her hands in the air.

Bunnicula went flying.

So did the dishes. Howie had
knocked into the kitchen table.

The dishes landed on the floor
with a crash.

Bunnicula landed on my back with
a thud.

The witch was cackling, but I kept going.

I had almost made it to the pet door with Bunnicula on my back when suddenly—two horrible creatures appeared!

"Hurry!" Chester screamed. "Go to the front door!"

As fast as I could I dashed to the front door.

Two terrible monsters were already there!

"We're trapped!" Chester moaned. "Doomed! About to be eaten by—"

CHAPTER 5

Halloween Surprise

Monroes?!

At that very moment the lights came back on.

"Mom!" Mr. Monroe cried. "What a surprise!"

"Grandma!" shouted Toby.

"You weren't supposed to come until tomorrow," said Pete.

"I thought I'd come early and surprise you," said Mr. Monroe's mother. "You know Halloween is my favorite holiday."

"Your costume and makeup are great," said Mrs. Monroe. "But what's wrong with your voice?"

"Oh, I have an awful cold. It makes me sound like a witch," Mr. Monroe's mother said, laughing.

"What happened to the lights?" Mr. Monroe asked.

"The power went out just as I got here. It must have been the storm."

"Did the storm break these dishes?" Mrs. Monroe asked, looking around at the mess.

"And why is Bunnicula riding Harold?" Pete wanted to know.

"I guess the animals got spooked in the dark," said Grandma Monroe. "Bunnicula was keeping me company while I made some hot apple cider. The next thing I knew, there was a stampede."

"Hot apple cider, my favorite!" Toby cried.

I turned to Chester. "Witch's brew, huh?"

"How do we know that's really Grandma Monroe?" he asked. "I mean, she might be a witch disguised as Grandma Monroe disguised as a witch."

"Now who's scared silly?" I said.

After the kitchen was tidy again, Grandma gave everyone treats. She gave the family some hot apple cider, and she gave us some special snacks she had brought with her.

They were yummy.

Things were just starting to get back to normal when Mr. Monroe said, "Oh, by the way, Mom, how was your flight?"

"A little bumpy, but I still say flying is the only way to go."

"Flying?" Howie gasped. "Look!"

We all stared at the broom she was holding.

"I was right! She *is* a witch!" Chester cried.

I don't know if Chester was right or not, but on this Halloween, I wasn't taking any chances.

"Move over, you two," I said. "It's going to be a long night."